This book belongs to

_____

_____

For Sebastian,
with thanks for all his help.

STERLING and the distinctive Sterling logo are registered trademarks
of Sterling Publishing Co., Inc.

Library of Congress Cataloging-in-Publication Data Available

Lot#:
2 4 6 8 10 9 7 5 3 1
12/09
Published by Sterling Publishing Co., Inc. in 2010, by arrangement with Gullane Children's Books.
387 Park Avenue South, New York, NY 10016
Text and Illustrations © 2000 by Charles Fuge
Distributed in Canada by Sterling Publishing
c/o Canadian Manda Group, 165 Dufferin Street
Toronto, Ontario, Canada M6K 3H6
Distributed in the United Kingdom by GMC Distribution Services
Castle Place, 166 High Street, Lewes, East Sussex, England BN7 1XU
Distributed in Australia by Capricorn Link (Australia) Pty. Ltd.
P.O. Box 704, Windsor, NSW 2756, Australia

Sterling ISBN 978-1-4027-7326-6

For information about custom editions, special sales, premium and
corporate purchases, please contact Sterling Special Sales
Department at 800-805-5489 or specialsales@sterlingpublishing.com.

Yip! Snap! Yap!

by Charles Fuge

STERLING

New York / London

Woof! Woof! Rruff!

Then turn the page
and join more pups
as they do their doggy stuff!

Dinner time for greedy dog . . . .

Careful of the guard dog . . .

Gruff!

Grrr!

G-ruff!

Don't catch fleas from itchy dog . . .

Scritch!
Scratch!
Scruff!

**Watch your feet!
It's yappy dog . . .**

Cool down with
a hot dog . . .

**Follow trails with
sniffer dog . . .**

Sniffle!
Snaffle!
Snoo!

Sing along with
puppy dogs . . .

Aroo!

Rowdy dog,
greedy dog,
sleepy dog,

Scratch!

guard dog,
itchy-scritchy-scratching dog,
yappy dog,
hot dog,
sniffer dog and
puppy dogs howling
at the moon . . .

Aroo!

Yap!

Other books by Charles Fuge

 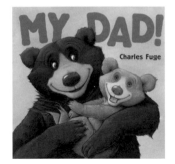 

This is the Way

My Dad!

I know A Rhino

and from the **Little Wombat** series

Sometimes I Like to Curl up in a Ball written by Vicki Churchill

Found You, Little Wombat! written by Angela MacAllister

Swim, Little Wombat, SWIM!

Where To, Little Wombat?

WATCH OUT! Little Wombat

The Adventures of Little Wombat
Four fun-filled Little Wombat adventures in a glorious bind-up.